Colin McNaughton

We're Off to Look for ALIENS

CANDLEWICK PRESS
CAMBRIDGE, MASSACHUSETTS

"Ah-ha!" said Dad.
"My alien book. Thank you,
Mr. Mailman."

It was Dad's new book, fresh from the printer. Dad writes children's books. He also draws the pictures. He says it's hard work, but he seems to spend an awful lot of time messing around.

"Tell me what you think,"
said Dad, handing us the book.
"I hope you like it."

Dad was too nervous
to watch us read, so he took
the dog for a walk.

This is what we read. . . .

"Well," said Dad, back from his walk, "what do you think of my alien book?"

"It's terrific, Dad," said my brother. "But there's a problem."

"What sort of problem?" asked Dad.

"Well," said Mom carefully, "it's a great book, and kids will love the pictures, but as for the story . . ."

"What's wrong with the story?"
asked Dad.

"It's wonderful!" said Mom quickly.
"But . . ."

"Yeah, Dad," I said. "It's really
great. It's just that kids tend to
like fairy tales and stuff, and
we were wondering . . .